the VERY WORST ever

iRSt DAY, WORSt DAY

BY ANDY NONAMUS
ILLUSTRATED BY AMY JINDRA

LITTLE SIMON

NEW YORK LONDON TORONTO SYDNEY NEW DELHI

LITTLE SIMON

An imprint of Simon & Schuster Children's Publishing Division

1230 Avenue of the Americas, New York, New York 10020

First Little Simon paperback edition January 2024

Copyright © 2024 by Simon & Schuster, LLC

Also available in a Little Simon hardcover edition

All rights reserved, including the right of reproduction in whole or in part in any form.

LITTLE SIMON is a registered trademark of Simon & Schuster, LLC, and associated colophon is a trademark of Simon & Schuster, LLC.

Simon & Schuster: Celebrating 100 Years of Publishing in 2024

For information about special discounts for bulk purchases, please contact Simon & Schuster Special Sales at 1-866-506-1949 or business@simonandschuster.com.

The Simon & Schuster Speakers Bureau can bring authors to your live event. For more information or to book an event contact the Simon & Schuster Speakers Bureau at 1-866-248-3049 or visit our website at www.simonspeakers.com.

Designed by Leslie Mechanic

The text of this book was set in Causten Round.

Manufactured in the United States of America 0924 LAK

10 9 8 7 6 5 4 3 2

Library of Congress Cataloging in Publication Data

Names: Nonamus, Andy, author. | Jindra, Amy, illustrator.

Title: First day, worst day / by Andy Nonamus ; illustrated by Amy Jindra.

Description: First Little Simon edition. | New York : Little Simon, 2024. |

Series: The very worst ever; 1 | Audience: Ages 5–9. | Summary: An elementary student, who wishes to remain anonymous, recounts the good and the bad of their first day of school.

Identifiers: LCCN 2023006576 (print) | LCCN 2023006577 (ebook) |

ISBN 9781665942201 (paperback) | ISBN 9781665942218 (hardcover) | ISBN 9781665942225 (ebook)

Subjects: CYAC: First day of school–Fiction. | Schools–Fiction. | Friendship–Fiction.

Classification: LCC PZ7.1.N6378 Fi 2024 (print) | LCC PZ7.1.N6378 (ebook) | DDC [Fic]–dc23

LC record available at https://lccn.loc.gov/2023006576

LC ebook record available at https://lccn.loc.gov/2023006577

CONTENTS

Hey, Reader!

Thanks for checking out my story.
Though I gotta warn you, I can't ever
let you know my real name or what
I look like. This may seem weird, but
trust me, it's very important that I
stay a secret.

Why? To protect myself! Seriously,
these stories are super embarrassing!

Plus, you might even know me already!
I could be in your class, on your
baseball team, in your ballet class, or
playing the tuba in your school band . . .
anywhere!

Hi!

For all you know I could be sitting next to you right now!

So I went ahead and scratched out my name and put a sticker on my face, so you don't have to. You're welcome.

Now, we can both enjoy reading all about my awkward life . . . if you're into that kind of thing.

Peace out!

MONDAYS, MAPLE SYRUP, AND MUTTS

If you ask me, Mondays get a bad rap.

Tuesdays have tacos. Saturdays have sleepovers and video games until dawn. But what have Mondays ever been good for?

I'll tell you: Mondays bring a fresh start. And for an unlucky kid like me, that's worth a thousand Saturdays.

Mondays mean last week's mistakes are in the past. Mondays come and hit the reset button on my cursed life.

This particular Monday marked the First Day of School. It was like a national holiday and Christmas morning all rolled into one. I got  new clothes, new sneakers, and best of all, a whole new town where absolutely no one knew me! I had gone to sleep as the Unluckiest

Boy Who Ever Lived. But today, I would wake up as the kid who—hold on. I hadn't actually woken up yet!

"███████, are you still in bed?!" Mom shouted from downstairs.

My eyes shot open and I threw the covers aside.

I looked at the clock, expecting to see the time. Only, there were no numbers on the screen. Just letters.

L-A-T-E silently flashed over and over again.

My alarm must have turned off! How? Who knows. Why? Well, because that's just my luck.

Mom called up again. "███████, you'd better hurry if you want jelly-bean pancakes!"

Jelly-bean pancakes?! I hit the ground running. Funny thing is, I almost hit the ground several times on my way to the kitchen. Once, when I tripped over my own pants. Twice, when I bumped into my bookshelf trying to slip on my shoes. And thrice, when I slipped on toothpaste after brushing my teeth.

This is what mornings are usually like for me.

"I'm coming, Ma!" I said, tracking minty globs behind me on the carpet.

I glided into the kitchen and saw a stack of colorful pancakes that was probably three feet tall.

"Why'd you let me oversleep?" I asked.

"I was on pancake duty, not wake-up duty," Mom said as she looked out the window. "Maybe I

should pack your breakfast to go."

"Why?" I asked.

"Because our driveway is about to become a drive-through lane," said Mom.

Outside I saw a yellow blur zoom past my house!

"THAT'S MY BUS!" I exclaimed.

I jumped up from the table and spilled maple syrup all over myself. This sticky day just got way stickier.

I had to catch that school bus or my Monday fresh start was doomed. So I bolted from my front door and screamed at the top of my lungs for it to ...

"WAAAAAAAAAAIT!!!"

But it was no use. The driver couldn't hear me over the sound of barking dogs.

Oh yeah, did I forget to mention the pack of dogs that were suddenly chasing me? That's what happens when you smell like maple syrup, I guess.

I ran faster. So did the dogs.

There was probably a good dog joke there somewhere, but I was too out of breath to think of one.

Suddenly, a minivan screeched around the corner and did a drift move straight out of an action movie.

The side door opened, and there was Mom, wearing her coolest sunglasses and driving gloves.

"Want a ride to school? You look *dog* tired." She giggled.

"Good ... dog joke ... Mom," I had to admit.

With my last ounce of energy left, I leapt into the van ... but so did all the dogs.

I was frozen with fear for a moment, but these mutts were friendly—a little too friendly. In one furry instant, they had licked every drop of syrup off me. I now looked like the human version of a wet mop.

There was no way this day could get any worse . . . right?

THE GHOST OF THE SCHOOL OFFICE

I walked through the front doors of New-School Elementary long after the late bell.

The pack of dogs followed me too, of course. All the way to the front office.

The moment I arrived at the front desk, I knew something was wrong.

It wasn't the normal plant by the window. It wasn't the normal clock on the wall. And it wasn't the bell on the desk, which—yes, you guessed it . . . was one hundred percent normal.

It was the desk itself. There was no one standing behind it.

But somehow, a voice came out of nowhere to say: "No pets allowed."

Who said that? I wondered.

I got on my tiptoes to try to peek over the countertop, but I was too short for it to make any difference.

Note to self: Ask Mom for bouncy shoes for my next birthday. Or maybe a ladder.

The cold voice interrupted my thoughts. "I said . . . no pets allowed."

"They're not my dogs," I told the voice. "It's a funny story–"

"I don't have time for funny stories," said the voice. "Neither do you. You're late. And *no–pets–allowed.*"

I turned to look at the pack of dogs. They all sat quietly with their tails

wagging and stared back at me.

"Uh . . . please go home, dogs?" I begged.

One by one, they left with their tails between their legs.

"Sorry," I whispered.

But then the Ghost of the School Office spoke again.

"Name?" it asked.

When ghosts ask you questions, you should probably give them the full story. And that's what I did.

"My name is ██████ █████," I said. "I was born on October the thirteenth. My favorite food is popcorn with ranch dressing on it. One time, I took such a strong sniff that a kernel went up my nose, and now I whistle when I smell stuff, like this."

I breathed in and whistled a long tune out. It sounded a bit like a pan flute. *FWEEEEEEEET!*

A long sigh came from the other side of the desk. I had angered the ghost! Then, footsteps.

Wait, ghosts don't have footsteps, do they?

A very, VERY short girl popped out from behind the desk. She was dressed in all black and wore creepy hair clips. In her hand was a piece of paper.

"Here is your late pass," she said.

"Thanks," I squeaked. "Wait, you look like a student. Do you work here?"

"I don't tell people my secrets," the girl said as she rolled her eyes. "And neither should you, Popcorn Nose. Now get to class . . . or I'll haunt you."

And just like that, the girl vanished behind the counter once again.

Of course, the first person I met at my new school might be a ghost.

Just my luck!

3

TIME
TO EXPLORE

My late pass read:

NAME: ▮▮▮▮▮▮▮▮ ▮▮▮▮▮▮▮▮

TIME OF ARRIVAL: LATE!

CLASSROOM: 31-Z

TEACHER: MR. HUGHES

EXCUSE: STUDENT WAS BUSY TELLING HIS LIFE
STORY TO A COMPLETE STRANGER. SOMETHING ABOUT
POPCORN AND WHISTLING. ALSO HE BROUGHT A PACK
OF WILD DOGS TO SCHOOL.

"They weren't wild," I grumbled. "They weren't even my dogs."

I looked up from the paper at the unfamiliar hallway that stretched in front of me.

There were no signs. No maps anywhere to show where you were.

Just closed door after closed door. Some had numbers on them, some did not.

I guess it was time to explore. I mean, one of these doors had to lead to my class, right?

I journeyed past classrooms 1 to 12 …

Interrupted classes in rooms 13 to 30 . . .

Got a few weird looks in the two bathrooms I peeked into . . .

But I couldn't find class 31-Z.

What I did find was myself, standing outside the school library.

I was alone. Confused. I needed help.

Surely some kind librarian would show me the way to class 31-Z. Or at least they could recommend a book on ancient history that might explain how a classroom could suddenly go extinct.

I stepped in and instantly heard, "HEADS UP!"

I looked to my left and saw a kind, old librarian. Then I looked to my right and saw . . . a bright orange ball hurtling straight at my face.

My first thought was: *Hey, that librarian is waving.*

My second thought was: *No, she's pointing at something behind me.*

The last thought I had before I got hit by a basketball to the face was: *Why say "HEADS UP!" when you should probably just say ... "DUCK DOWN!"?*

4

THE LIBRARY GYM AND JAKE GOLD

There I was, on my back, staring up at a crowd.

I tried playing it off like it was no big deal to get hit in the face by a basketball traveling a million miles per hour. But they'd all seen me get thwacked. I'd be the talk of the school in no time.

A hush fell over the library as a muscle-bound boy took a knee next to me. He had hair like Thor and a deep, manly voice. The bright lights behind him made him look like an angel. But instead of a halo, all I saw him hold up was his hand.

"How many fingers do you see?" he asked.

Wow. Even his fingers had muscles.

"Three," I responded.

He faced the crowd with a grin. "His brain works, everyone! He's okay!"

The others cheered as the angel-kid helped me to my feet.

"The name's Gold." He swished his
majestic hair. "Jake Gold."

I tried swishing my own hair back,
but all I wound up doing was getting
hair in my own eye. "I'm ▓▓▓▓▓▓▓."

A mustached man in short shorts suddenly appeared, blowing a whistle that hung around his neck. This had to be the school's gym coach. "Everything okay?" he boomed. "Don't be frightened. I'm the librarian, Mr. Bookman."

This was the librarian?

I looked over at the kindly, old woman who'd waved at me before I got hit.

"If you're the librarian, then who's that?" I asked.

"That's Coach Olympia," Jake said matter-of-factly.

The old woman pointed at me and said, "Next time you see a ball coming . . . dodge it, rookie!"

This new school kept getting weirder and weirder.

"I thought this was the library?" I asked.

We were clearly surrounded by stacks of books. But in the center of the room, there was a basketball court with hoops. Some kids were reading at tables, while other kids were playing basketball.

"Welcome to the library-gym," Jake said.

Mr. Bookman blew his whistle again.

"Gold, take the new guy to the nurse."

"On it!" Jake exclaimed.

He jumped into action and started running in place so quickly that his sneakers were a blur!

"Should we race to the nurse's office?" Jake asked.

"I don't really do sports," I told him. "My legs only have one speed: snail."

But Jake didn't believe me.

"How do you know that if you don't really do sports?" he asked. "Ready . . . ?"

I was really sweating now. "Ready for what?"

"Set . . ." Jake's legs blurred even more as he ran in place. How was this possible?!

"No, not set–" I practically begged.

"GO!" And like a jet taking off, Jake flew down the hall at turbo speed.

I had no choice but to jog after him. Normally, this would have been a deal breaker for me. But once I saw kids start using the tables as shields for the basketballs, I knew I needed to head out before I got head-smashed again.

5

NURSE DOC
AND THE GOOP

If shoes could talk, then mine were definitely saying: *Ouch! Stop doing this... WHATEVER you call this!*

(I believe it was called "jogging.")

At least, that's what I thought I was doing. My feet moved, but I wasn't getting any closer to Jake. In fact, he was shrinking away into the distance.

I slowed down at the water fountain for a drink. Sure, it was tap water, but it tasted amazing after that epic run I'd just completed . . . of six whole feet!

"Thought I lost you there," a voice called.

I turned around with water dribbling down my chin. It was Jake!

"I totally beat you to the nurse's office," he said.

"But you came back for me?" I asked in shock.

"Yep," said Jake with a wink. "Must be your lucky day."

I seriously doubted that.

Unlike the library-gym, the nurse's office was just the nurse's office. No combo nurse's janitor's closet or nurse's cafeteria.

But it was empty—except for the nurse, of course.

She signaled for me to sit down.

"Mr. Gold . . . ," she said to Jake. "Already hit someone with a ball today?"

"It was an accident, Nurse Doc!" Jake replied. ▨▨▨▨▨ doesn't know the meaning of 'heads up.'"

(Yes, the nurse's name was actually Nurse Doc. Weird, right?!)

"Not everyone is as athletic as the famous Golds," Nurse Doc said. "Jake's parents are Olympic gold medalists. They can do pretty much anything."

Whoa—now I understood Jake's speed. It was literally in his DNA!

"Time for a cranium exam," Nurse Doc said.

Then she checked my head for lumps. When she didn't find any, she pulled out some goop and slathered it into my hair. It smelled awful. The gunk, not my hair.

"What's the damage?" I asked after a few minutes.

"Well," said Nurse Doc, "you're going to live. But I may need to use ice cubes and peanut butter to get this gunk out of your hair."

Out of nowhere, a new voice said, "Be a doll and get me more ice, please? My face is still puffy."

I jumped. I thought we were the only ones here! Was there a ghost in the nurse's office, too?

"For the last time, your face is not puffy, Regina," Nurse Doc said. "Now, please, I have a real patient to help."

"Ooh, another patient!" the voice exclaimed. "Forget the ice. Be a dear and open the curtain for me? I need to make my big entrance!"

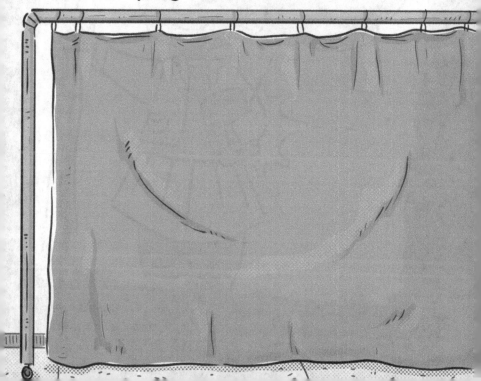

6

ZOMBIES, ROOSTERS, AND REGINA

As the curtains parted next to Nurse Doc's desk, we were hit with flashing lights and the sound of applause. Was there an audience hidden in here?

No.

But there was a tablet blinking the name ...

REGINA DU LAR!

The girl holding the tablet had perfectly done hair and shiny clothes. She sparkled like a famous someone. The girl bowed and said, "It is I...Regina du Lar!"

"Hold on. Like, THE Du Lar?!" I asked. "As in Du Lar Video Game Emporium?"

"That's me! Well, that's my family's company, I mean," she said as she gave me a handshake. "Always nice to meet a fan."

I shook her hand for a really long time. Because, like she guessed, I was a fan.

"I own all your family's games. *Zombie Karts*, *Zombie Kitchen*, *Zombie Wrestling*," I babbled on with excitement.

"Sounds like you just love zombies." She laughed.

"Zombies are way too scary for me," Jake admitted. "I like games with cute animals. Like . . . *Enchanted Barnyard Dance Party!*"

Regina's mouth dropped. "That's MY favorite game too! Let's play while we wait for your goop to dry."

Then she pulled out two more tablets for us.

I didn't really like video games where you had to dance around with silly characters, but my new friends seemed to like them a lot.

Hey, wait a sec . . . did I just say "friends"? Was I making FRIENDS?

This was a first. I wasn't really the kind of kid who made friends. You had to be confident and cool to meet people. I mean, I have met other kids before ... but it was usually when they were laughing ... at me.

As it turned out, I just needed to find my rhythm. Maybe my luck was changing.

I didn't want to jinx it, so I did what anyone would do. I imitated a chicken and flapped my arms up and down to the music. It was good enough to earn fifty style points for my Rappin' Rooster character.

"Fancy flappin'," said Nurse Doc, who reappeared to check me one last time. "Your goop's dry. No need for PB and ice."

I touched my hair carefully. "Can I ask what the goop was for?"

"Fleas," Nurse Doc replied. "Your hair was covered in fleas. I've never seen so many. What happened?"

My mind flashed back to the dogs from this morning.

"It's a long story." I sighed. Nurse Doc gave us each hall passes and some not-so-friendly medical advice. "Stop flappin' and get to class!"

Oh no! I was having such a good time dancing that I forgot my whole reason for being at school in the first place!

"Aww, I know that look," Regina teased. "No need to beg. I'll join your weird little quest to find ... wherever it is you're looking for."

"Umm, my class," I said. "I'm looking for classroom 31-Z."

"Just follow me," she said. "I know all the hottest spots in school."

As we followed Regina out of the room, Jake nudged me. "Better keep up. I don't know where anything is around here. We can't lose her!"

7

DANGER, MOUSETRAPS, AND MEATBALLS

Luckily, Regina kept a steady pace.

"*Locating classroom 31-Z!*" her tablet announced.

On the screen was a 3D map of the school with a line tracking us.

"*Follow this path,*" the voice added.

"I didn't know we could download a school app," Jake whispered to me.

"I just follow everyone around. It works most of the time!"

We followed the map past every classroom . . . every bathroom . . . and every locker. Finally, the app chimed and then announced, *"Destination reached."*

Our "destination" was a locker with no number on it, just graffiti scribbled on the outside. It read: NOTHING TO SEE HERE.

"Well, that's not weird at all," I joked.

"Disagree, bro," Jake said. He didn't get my sarcasm. "It's definitely weird."

The tablet said, "*Spin the numbers: thirty-one, thirty-one, thirty-one.*"

Regina looked up at me. I looked at Jake.

Jake looked at Regina and said, "Okay, we've all looked at each other. Now what?"

Since it was my quest that brought us here, I knew I had to be the one to unlock the mysterious door and peek inside. So I swallowed my fear and spun the combination three times. 31...31...31...

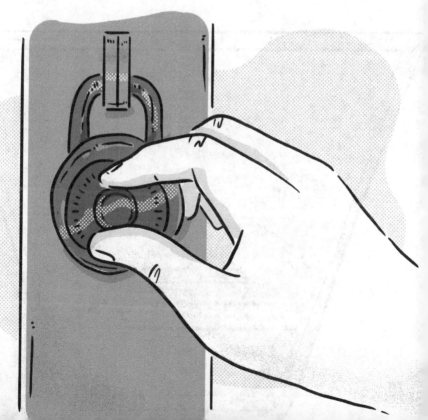

With a click, the door slowly opened. This was no ordinary locker. There were no shelves or books inside. Only a dark staircase.

A staircase that went down.

"I don't really do creepy stuff. Call me when you're done investigating," Regina said.

Suddenly an alarm went off. It was coming from the tablet. *"WARNING! STRANGER APPROACHING!"*

What were we supposed to do?

The screen showed a new dot moving toward us!

There was nowhere else to go . . . but down.

"I've got this!" said Jake as he went into full "Jake mode" and scooped me and Regina up. Then he squeezed the three of us into that locker and carried us down the dark staircase, revealing a tunnel that went under the school!

While dangling sideways in Jake's arm, I saw things. Weird things. We passed a room with a lizard in an aquarium. Another room had tons of mousetraps that surrounded one lone meatball sub. Then, a room with a . . . pirate's treasure chest? And was that a ROBOT?

What kind of school was this?

"What do I do now?"
Jake shouted, still running.

On cue, the tablet said,
"Turn right, then right, then
right, then right, then
go upstairs."

Jake took every
turn until we found
a staircase, which
he flew up. Then
we found a
door, which he
leapt out and
slammed shut
behind him."

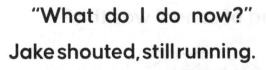

Strangely, it was the same locker
door from before.

"Did we just go in a circle?" I asked.

"You weren't supposed to see that,"
a stormy voice said.

Jake turned us around
and we saw someone
else standing there.

A figure hidden in the shadows.
Dark. Mysterious.

And very, VERY short.

GLOOM, GLINDA, AND BAD HANDWRITING

We were all too scared to move as the mysterious stranger stepped out of the shadows.

First we saw only black shoes.

Then two ghostly pale hands.

And finally ... a skull hair clip?!

"I know you!" I exclaimed.

This was no terrifying stranger.

It was the maybe-ghost-girl from the front office!

Turns out, there was nothing "ghostly" about her. She just had a very spooky fashion sense. Everything she wore was dark, even the sash that read HALL MONITOR.

"Busted," she said. "I have to write you all up for wandering the halls without a pass."

Regina crossed her arms. "We have passes, Glinda!"

GLINDA! The ghost girl had a name!

As we handed over our passes, I said, "So you work in the office and you're the hall monitor—what don't you do?"

"I have zero limits," Glinda said without a hint of excitement. "I can't be stopped."

"Woot-woot!" Regina cheered, raising her hands up and down. "Girl power!"

Jake tried to join in. "Woo, girl power! So . . . can we talk about the locker that's actually a secret tunnel?"

"No," Glinda answered. "Can't you read? There's nothing to see here."

Then she handed our hall passes back.

"Here's your problem," Glinda told me. "You want room 312, not room 31-Z. Where'd you get 31-Z from?"

I snapped. "I GOT IT FROM YOU! FROM THE NOTE YOU WROTE ME THIS MORNING!"

"Hmmm." Glinda thought it over. "You must have read it wrong."

I was about to really lose it now . . . but then Regina had a better idea.

"Maybe you could help us find 312, Glinda?" she asked. "You are the hall monitor, after all."

Glinda sighed heavily. "Fine."

Glinda led us to a door that was tucked around a corner and blocked by another row of lockers.

Coming from behind that door . . . was a glow.

"Classroom 312." Glinda motioned to the door like it was no big deal. (You know, as if it wasn't GLOWING like a science experiment gone wrong!)

Jake looked at the classroom door and gave a giant gasp. "Hold on a second . . . this is MY classroom!"

"How did you not realize that earlier?!" I asked.

Glinda stayed cool. "Do you want
to ask questions? Or do you want to
start your first day before the last
bell rings?"

9

SPARE UNDERWEAR AND MY MOM

RIIIIIIIIIIIING!!!

Every single door opened at the sound of the final bell, and it hit me. I'd officially missed my first day of school ... WHILE I WAS AT SCHOOL.

And if that wasn't bad enough, we were about to be flattened by students flooding the hallway.

I hid behind Glinda, who led us through the tidal wave of kids like a sea captain sailing through rough waters.

We eventually made our way through a door.

THE door. Room 312.

"Student delivery," Glinda said.

I looked up at the room around us.

There wasn't anything special about classroom 312, except that it was filled with lights from a strange orb resting on the teacher's desk. It glowed with flickering blue sparkles.

The teacher put the orb back into his desk drawer and greeted us with a curious look.

"Can I help you?" he asked.

"I found him," Glinda said, pointing to me. "Your missing student."

The man looked at me and smiled. "Ah, you must be ███████. We heard you'd been dragged away by wild dogs."

Great, I thought. *Even my new teacher knows my life's gone to the dogs.*

The man introduced himself. "I'm Mr. Hughes."

"I'm ████████," I said. "Reporting for my first day of school."

"Excellent," said Mr. Hughes. "Let's show you to your new home, even if the first day of school is done."

Then he pointed to a desk by the window.

My desk. It still had that new-desk smell.

"I'm sorry I missed everything!" I confessed. "But you wouldn't believe the epic journey I've been on to find this place."

"Hey, at least your journey is over," Mr. Hughes said.

Except, it wasn't.

As I sat down, an announcement came over the intercom.

" ▮▮▮▮▮▮, please come to the front office. Your mom is on the phone. She says that it is urgent, like the time you needed her to bring you new underwear because the toilet overflowed."

There it was. A message blasted for the whole school to hear.

Laughter echoed through the hallways. It followed me everywhere like a curse.

Even at my new, weird school.

10

FIRST DAY, WORST DAY

I took the "scenic route" to the office.

That just meant I took the longest way possible to avoid seeing anyone who might laugh at me. This involved walking around the block and sneaking back onto school property through a giant mail slot that was reserved for oversized boxes.

As I poked my head up above the letters and packages, I saw it. The school phone.

I picked it up and asked, "Mom, what's wrong?"

Turns out, nothing! (Whew!)

"I have to work late, honey," Mom explained. "Make sure you catch the bus, or you will have to walk home, and the raccoons might come out. I know how afraid you are of those little critters."

That was all I needed to cap off this banner first day. Night of the Rabid Raccoons! Not again.

"Okay, Mom," I said.

I was not looking forward to taking another "scenic route" home by myself. I'd seen enough.

Time to crawl back through the mail slot.

"What are you doing?" Glinda asked.

I turned to find Regina, Jake, and Glinda waiting outside the office.

"Are you guys here to laugh about the underpants announcement too?" I asked.

"No," said Regina. "We wanted to make sure you were okay."

"My mom has to work late," I explained as I headed outside. "And the bus probably left, so it looks like I'm walking home."

"Why walk when you can jog?" Jake suggested, his legs already moving.

Regina turned to me in a fabulous swirl. "Why jog when you can...LIMO?"

BEEP-BEEP!

As if on cue, a shiny limousine pulled up outside.

"Who wants a ride home?" said Regina.

"Are you serious?!" I gasped.

"She never jokes about limos," Glinda said with a straight face.

The chauffeur opened the door for us and I hopped inside with a big, dumb grin on my face.

It was my first time riding in a real-life limo. There was music playing and a cooler filled with juice and snacks. There was even a popcorn machine!

Glinda handed me some and said, "Just don't sniff it, okay?"

"This...is...AMAZING!" I exclaimed.

And it was. But looking around, I realized ... the snacks weren't the best thing about the limo. *They* were–the other people riding inside it with me.

I cracked a smile as I watched them giggling. For once, the laughs weren't directed at me.

"Time for a selfie!" cheered Regina. "Everyone say, 'First Day, Worst Day!'"

Wouldn't you know it? I messed that up too. As the camera flashed, I accidentally said, "First Day, *Best* Day!"

(Which I don't think was an accident at all.)

HERE'S A PEEK AT
████████'S
NEXT
ADVENTURE!

When I say "class clown," you might think of a silly kid from school. They might even make animal noises during class. *Caw-caw,* they'd say, like a toucan. Or *ooooh-ahhh-ah-ah* like a monkey.

Hilarious, right?

An excerpt from *Pop Goes the Carnival*

Yeah ... this wasn't like that.

I walked into classroom 312 to see a class clown ... but it wasn't even human! It was a balloon with a red nose and a teardrop on its face. Its tiny shoes had weights, so it always stood upright. Even if you threw your backpack at it, the clown would bounce back up with its beady little eyes.

And just my luck, it was right next to my desk.

I made my way over carefully and tried to sit down without making eye contact. But the moment I tried to scoot

An excerpt from *Pop Goes the Carnival*

my desk up just a tad bit, the clown rocked down and booped the top of my head.

"AGH!" I shouted, trying to get away.

Mr. Hughes, my teacher, grinned in front of the board. "Ah, ████████, I see you've met Happy."

"This thing's name is Happy?" I squeaked.

"I got you, bro!" said a voice across the classroom.

It was Jake Gold. He was best at gym class and best at being one of my new best friends.

An excerpt from *Pop Goes the Carnival*